HEROES OF BLACK HISTORY

TONI MORRISON

I0869297

BY JANEY LEVY

Gareth Stevens
PUBLISHING

Please visit our website, www.garethstevens.com. For a free color catalog of all our high-quality books, call toll free 1-800-542-2595 or fax 1-877-542-2596.

Library of Congress Cataloging-in-Publication Data
Names: Levy, Janey, author.
Title: Toni Morrison / Janey Levy.
Description: New York : Gareth Stevens Publishing, [2021] | Series: Heroes of black history | Includes index.
Identifiers: LCCN 2019047966 | ISBN 9781538258040 (library binding) | ISBN 9781538258026 (paperback) | ISBN 9781538258033 (6 Pack) | ISBN 9781538258057 (ebook)
Subjects: LCSH: Morrison, Toni--Juvenile literature. | African American novelists--Biography--Juvenile literature.
Classification: LCC PS3563.O8749 Z7526 2021 | DDC 813/.54--dc23
LC record available at https://lccn.loc.gov/2019047966

First Edition

Published in 2021 by
Gareth Stevens Publishing
111 East 14th Street, Suite 349
New York, NY 10003

Copyright © 2021 Gareth Stevens Publishing

Designer: Laura Bowen
Editor: Monika Davies

Photo credits: Cover, p. 1 (Toni Morrison) Deborah Feingold/Contributor/Corbis Entertainment/Getty Images; cover, pp. 1-32 (background image) Paramonov Alexander/Shutterstock.com; p. 5 Newsday LLC/Contributor/NewsdayRM/Getty Images; p. 7 (top) Foxtod/Wikimedia Commons; p. 7 (bottom) AlexWooledge/Wikimedia Commons; p. 9 N8hawk/Wikimedia Commons; p. 11 Evelyn Hockstein/For The Washington Post via Getty Images; p. 13 FREDERIC J. BROWN/Contributor/AFP/Getty Images; p. 14 (Young) Americus55/Wikimedia Commons; p. 14 (Carmichael) GPRamirez5/Wikimedia Commons; p. 15 (Washington, D.C.) Orhan Cam/Shutterstock.com; p. 15 (Houston) Sean Pavone/Shutterstock.com; p. 15 (map) Ad_hominem/Shutterstock.com; pp. 17, 24 Jack Mitchell/Contributor/Archive Photos/Getty Images; p. 19 debra millet/Shutterstock.com; p. 20 RIANbot/Wikimedia Commons; p. 21 Evening Standard/Stringer/Hulton Archive/Getty Images; p. 23 Archive Photos/Stringer/Archive Photos/Getty Images; p. 25 UAlbany/Wikimedia Commons; p. 26 Fairfax Media Archives/Contributor/Fairfax Media Archive/Getty Images; p. 27 Harpo Films/Hulton Archive/Moviepix/Getty Images; p. 28 Rena Schild/Shutterstock.com

All rights reserved. No part of this book may be reproduced in any form without permission in writing from the publisher, except by a reviewer.

Printed in the United States of America

Some of the images in this book illustrate individuals who are models. The depictions do not imply actual situations or events.

CPSIA compliance information: Batch #CS20GS. For further information contact Gareth Stevens, New York, New York at 1-800-542-2595

Find us on

CONTENTS

Words in the glossary appear in **bold** type the first time they are used in the text.

MEET TONI MORRISON

If you like to read, you may have heard of Toni Morrison. She was one of the most celebrated writers of the late 20th century and early 21st century. She wrote 11 **novels**, as well as children's books, books of **essays**, and plays.

Toni won many awards, or prizes. In 1977, she received the National Book **Critics** Award for her book *Song of Solomon*. She also won the 1988 Pulitzer Prize for her book *Beloved*. In 1993, Toni was the first black woman to be awarded the Nobel Prize in **Literature**. Inside this book, you'll discover more about this talented writer.

NOBEL PRIZE IN LITERATURE

The Nobel Prize in Literature is awarded to "the person who shall have produced in the field of literature the most outstanding work in an ideal direction." The prize isn't awarded for a single book, but for a writer's whole body, or collection, of writing work.

Toni wrote about black people's experiences living in the United States. She was especially interested in the experiences of black women.

GROWING UP

On February 18, 1931, the child who would become Toni Morrison was born in Lorain, Ohio. Lorain was a racially integrated community, or a community that welcomed all races of people. Her parents, George and Ella Ramah Wofford, named her Chloe Ardelia.

Chloe grew up in a home that deeply loved and valued black **culture**. Songs, tales, and stories based on black life in the South filled her home and shaped her life. When Chloe started school, she went to an integrated school. She later said, "When I was in first grade, nobody thought I was **inferior**. I was the only black in the class and the only child who could read."

TONI'S PARENTS

Toni's parents moved from different states in the South to Ohio. They moved from the South in order to find a better life with more opportunities. Toni's father was a shipyard welder who worked at several jobs to provide for his family. Her mother did domestic work and was also an active member of her church.

This is downtown Lorain, Ohio, as it looks today. The city is still a diverse community, as it was when the Woffords moved there.

Chloe joined the Catholic Church when she was 12. It was a customary, or common, practice in the church for a baby to be given a saint's name. Since Chloe joined the church when she was 12, she took a saint's name then. She chose the name *Anthony*, and became Chloe Anthony Wofford.

Chloe went to Lorain High School and cleaned for a family after school. She earned $2 a week, giving $1 to her mom and keeping the other dollar for buying candy. Chloe was an excellent student, studying Latin and reading a variety of literature. In 1949, she graduated from high school with honors.

YOUNG CHLOE'S INTERESTS

As a child, Chloe dreamed of becoming a dancer like Maria Tallchief, a famous American ballet dancer. Unsurprisingly for someone who'd become a writer, Chloe also loved to read. Some of her favorite writers included Jane Austen and Russian authors such as Leo Tolstoy and Fyodor Dostoyevski.

LORAIN HIGH SCHOOL

Chloe was also on her high school's debate team and a member of the yearbook staff.

BECOMING TONI

Chloe went to Howard University in Washington, DC, where she made English her major field of study. Howard University is a historically black university. At college, Chloe discovered her first name was difficult, or hard, for other students to pronounce correctly. Chloe decided to take her saint's name—Anthony—and create a new name for herself. She began calling herself Toni.

Toni joined the university theater group and acted in plays. The group went on tours to the South, and Toni saw firsthand what **segregated** life was like for black people there.

MORE EDUCATION

Toni graduated with a degree in English from Howard University in 1953. She then attended Cornell University in Ithaca, New York. She received a master's degree in English from Cornell in 1955. She was then offered a job teaching at another college, and the next stage of her life began.

Historically black colleges and universities were established to provide education for black people when they weren't allowed to go to other colleges and universities.

A TEACHING CAREER

Toni's first teaching position was at Texas Southern University in Houston. Just like Howard University, Texas Southern University is a historically black university. Toni taught there for two years. While she was there, she encountered the idea of black culture and history as something one could study.

Black culture and history had, of course, been an important part of Toni's life growing up. At Howard University, there had been little **academic** attention paid to black culture and history. But at Texas Southern University, black culture and history was celebrated, and Toni began to see them as subjects for serious study.

HISTORICALLY BLACK COLLEGES AND UNIVERSITIES

Black churches were largely responsible for founding the first colleges for black people. From 1861 to 1900, more than 90 such colleges and universities were established. The first one founded after the **American Civil War** was Shaw University in Raleigh, North Carolina. The early colleges and universities trained students to become teachers and preachers.

Texas Southern University was founded in 1927 and is one of the largest historically black universities in America.

In 1957, Toni returned to Howard University to teach. The years at Howard were an important period in Toni's life. She met people who would become key figures in the civil rights movement. This was a time period in U.S. history in which black people fought for equal civil rights, or the freedoms granted to us by law. Among the people she met were Andrew Young, a future politician, as well as Stokely Carmichael, a political **activist**.

Toni also began writing seriously. She joined a small writers group. Every week at her group's meeting, she had to have a story or poem written and ready to share with the group.

STOKELY CARMICHAEL

ANDREW YOUNG

BLUE EYES

Toni wrote a story for her writers group that she'd later turn into her first novel. It was about a young black girl who prayed for blue eyes. The young black girl wished for blue eyes because everything she saw in her day-to-day life sent her the message that being beautiful meant being white and having blue eyes.

IMPORTANT PLACES IN YOUNG TONI'S LIFE

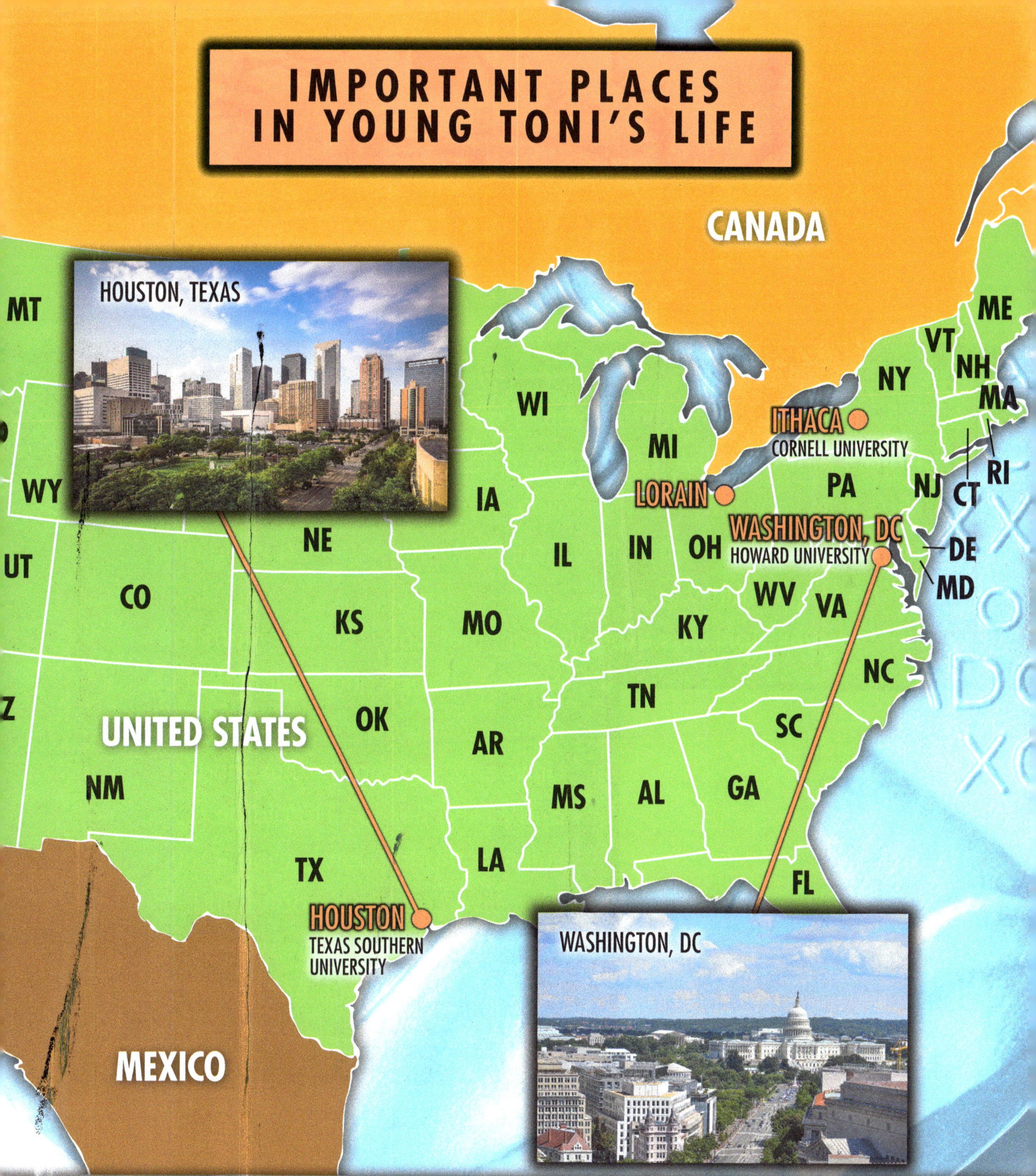

This map shows places where Toni lived, worked, or studied in her younger days. Her experiences in these cities shaped her life and future.

LOVE AND LOSS

In 1958, Toni married a young architect from Jamaica named Harold Morrison. She took his last name, which gave her the name she's now known by—Toni Morrison. Toni and Harold's first son, Harold Ford, was born in 1961. Toni continued teaching while also caring for her family.

In 1964, Toni was expecting another baby. But her marriage wasn't a happy one. Toni ended up quitting her teaching job at Howard University, leaving her husband, and taking her son Harold on a summer trip through Europe. Toni then divorced her husband and returned to Lorain, Ohio, where she briefly moved in with her parents.

WHAT HAPPENED?

What happened to cause Toni's marriage to end? She didn't talk about her marriage often. She hinted that her husband wished she would fill a **traditional** role in their household and perhaps hoped Toni wouldn't work outside of their home. Toni knew she couldn't be happy living that way.

In 1964, Toni's second son, Slade Kevin, was born in Ohio. This photograph shows Toni (center), Harold Ford (top), and Slade Kevin (bottom).

THE WRITTEN WORD

Toni found a new job in Syracuse, New York, in the fall of 1964. With this new job, her life was all about the written word. She became a textbook editor for the publisher Random House. An editor is someone who corrects or improves a writer's work or changes it to fit the publisher's style.

Life as a single mother could be hard. While she worked all day, the housekeeper took care of her young sons. Toni cooked dinner and played with her sons in the evening. Then, after her sons went to bed, she wrote.

WHAT'S A PUBLISHER'S STYLE?

Every publisher has a style, or a special way of structuring the content in their books. A publisher's style covers a variety of elements about how things are written. For example, a publisher's style decides if contractions are used in their books. This decides if one writes "what's" or "what is."

Toni lived in Syracuse for around two years. While living in the city, she began to turn the short story she'd written in her writers group into her first novel, *The Bluest Eye.*

Toni was then transferred, or moved, to Random House's offices in New York City. There, she began editing books written by famous black people, including the **autobiographies** of boxer Muhammad Ali and political activist Angela Davis.

During her early years as an editor, Toni was still writing and trying to get her first novel published. *The Bluest Eye* was finally published in 1970. Toni was 39 years old at the time. *The Bluest Eye* didn't sell especially well, but Toni's career as a writer had officially begun. Many critics gave the book high praise, making the start a promising one.

BLACK FICTION

Toni was especially interested in publishing black fiction, or stories. She said, "I look very hard for black fiction because I want to participate [take part] in developing a canon of black work." Toni was stating she wanted to help create a collection of written work by black writers that would be accepted as important literature.

ANGELA DAVIS

Toni helped edit Muhammad Ali's autobiography, *The Greatest: My Own Story,* which was released in 1975.

TEACHER AND WRITER

Toni taught at the State University College in Purchase, New York from 1971 to 1972. She was also working on her second novel. *Sula* was published in 1973, and, unlike *The Bluest Eye,* it was successful with the public as well as with critics. Part of the novel was published in a popular magazine. It could be ordered through a book club. *Sula* was nominated, or suggested, for the National Book Award.

Toni also taught at Yale University in New Haven, Connecticut from 1976 to 1977. She was writing her third novel, *Song of Solomon,* at the same time.

ABOUT *SULA* AND *SONG OF SOLOMON*

Sula tells the story of the lifelong friendship between two black women set in their home of Medallion, Ohio. In *Song of Solomon,* the story of four generations of a black family, is told by a male figure who is trying to figure out who he is. The story is set in a Michigan town.

Toni continued to work at Random House during this time. In this period of her life, she was doing three jobs: editing, teaching, and writing.

Song of Solomon was published in 1977. It's the book that made Toni famous. *Song of Solomon* won both the National Book Critics Circle Award and the American Academy and Institute of Arts and Letters Award. In 1980, President Jimmy Carter chose Toni to join the National Council on the Arts.

Toni published her fourth novel, *Tar Baby*, in 1981. That same year, her picture appeared on the cover of *Newsweek* magazine—a sign of just how famous and successful she'd become. In 1983, Toni left her job as an editor at Random House so she could spend more time on her writing.

TONI WRITES A PLAY

Toni wrote her first play while she was in Albany, New York. The play was called *Dreaming Emmett*. It was based on true events involving Emmett Till, a black Mississippi teenager who was killed by white men in the 1950s. The white men killed Emmett because they thought he whistled at a white woman.

Toni continued teaching. She started teaching at the State University of New York at Albany in 1984.

In 1987, what many consider to be Toni's greatest book was published: *Beloved*. *Beloved* was inspired by the true story of an escaped slave named Margaret Garner. When Margaret was about to be recaptured, she decided to kill her baby daughter rather than let her grow up as a slave. *Beloved* won a major award called the Pulitzer Prize, which recognizes outstanding accomplishment in American letters, or written work. The book was later made into a movie.

Toni wrote many more books after *Beloved*. Her list of novels include *Jazz*, a story that takes place in 1920s Harlem in New York City, and *Paradise*, a story about the all-black town of Ruby, Oklahoma.

TONI'S CHILDREN'S BOOKS

Toni didn't just write novels for adults. She also worked with her son Slade to co-write several children's books. A diverse group of characters was always featured in their books. Their book list includes the *Who's Got Game?* series, *The Big Box*, *The Book About Mean People*, *Peeny Butter Fudge*, and *Please, Louise*.

Oprah Winfrey played Sethe, the main character and escaped slave in the movie of *Beloved.*

THE GREAT AMERICAN NOVELIST

Toni kept earning honors. *The New York Times* often listed her books as best sellers among the American public. A best seller is a book with very high sales. *Time* magazine put Toni on its cover, naming her "The Great American Storyteller." In 1993, she became the first black woman to receive the Nobel Prize in Literature, one of the highest honors for a writer.

Toni was also awarded the National Humanities Medal in 2000. President Barack Obama awarded her the U.S. Presidential Medal of Freedom in 2012. A talented writer respected and loved by many, Toni died in 2019 at age 88.

TONI'S NOBEL PRIZE

The Swedish Academy is the body that awards the Nobel Prizes. In choosing Toni to receive the Nobel Prize in Literature, it spoke of the "**visionary** and poetic" qualities of her novels. The Academy said that in Toni's work she "gives life to an essential [important] aspect of American reality."

OBAMA AND MORRISON

A TIMELINE OF TONI'S LIFE

FEBRUARY 18, 1931 Chloe Ardelia Wofford is born.

1943 Chloe joins the Roman Catholic Church and becomes Chloe Anthony Wofford.

1949–1953 Chloe goes to Howard University and changes her name to Toni.

1953–1955 Toni goes to Cornell University.

1955–1957 Toni teaches at Southern Texas University.

1957 Toni starts teaching at Howard University.

1958 Toni gets married and becomes Toni Morrison.

1964 Toni quits her job at Howard and leaves her husband. She begins a career as an editor at Random House.

1970 Her first novel, *The Bluest Eye*, is published.

1973 Her second novel, *Sula*, is published.

1977 Her third novel, *Song of Solomon*, is published and wins awards.

1981 Her fourth novel, *Tar Baby*, is published.

1983 Toni quits her job at Random House to write more.

1987 Her greatest book, *Beloved*, is published. It wins the Pulitzer Prize and is made into a movie.

1993 Toni wins the Nobel Prize in Literature.

2012 Toni receives the U.S. Presidential Medal of Freedom.

2019 Toni dies.

Toni spent many years writing books that inspired others. She once said, "If there's a book that you want to read, but it hasn't been written yet, then you must write it."

GLOSSARY

academic: belonging to schools and education

activist: one who acts strongly in support of or against an issue or cause

American Civil War: a war fought from 1861 to 1865 in the United States between the Union (the Northern states) and the Confederacy (the Southern states)

autobiography: a book written by someone about their life

critic: someone who gives opinions about books, movies, or other types of art

culture: the beliefs and ways of life of a group of people

essay: a piece of writing

inferior: of less importance or value

literature: written works that are believed to be excellent and to have enduring importance

novel: a lengthy written story about imaginary people and events

segregated: a state of forced separation of races or classes

traditional: having to do with long-practiced customs

visionary: having a unique and powerful imagination

FOR MORE INFORMATION

BOOKS

Morrison, Toni and Slade Morrison. *The Big Box.* New York, NY: Jump At The Sun, 1999.

Randolph, Joanne. *African American Artists & Writers.* New York, NY: Enslow Publishing, 2018.

Wilson, Jamia. *Young, Gifted, and Black: Meet 52 Black Heroes from Past and Present.* London, UK: Wide Eyed Editions, 2018.

WEBSITES

Biography: Toni Morrison - Novelist
www.theheroinecollective.com/toni-morrison/
Learn more about Toni's life story on this website.

Chloe Anthony Wofford "Toni" Morrison (1931 – 2019)
www.blackpast.org/african-american-history/morrison-chloe-anthony-wofford-nee-toni-morrison-1931/
Read more about Toni's books and plays here.

Toni Morrison: A Life in Pictures
www.theguardian.com/books/gallery/2019/aug/06/toni-morrison-a-life-in-pictures
Find pictures of Toni throughout her life here.

Publisher's note to educators and parents: Our editors have carefully reviewed these websites to ensure that they are suitable for students. Many websites change frequently, however, and we cannot guarantee that a site's future contents will continue to meet our high standards of quality and educational value. Be advised that students should be closely supervised whenever they access the internet.

INDEX